DATE DUE

OCT 1 5 2008		
NOV 0 2008		
NOV 1 2 2008		
NOV 1 9 2008		
MAR 1 8 2009		
NOV 0 4 2009		
OCT 2 0 2010		
NOV 2 2 2010		
MAR 0 2 2011		
JAN 2 5 2012		
SEP 2 6 2012		
DE '14		
JA 0 8 '14		
MY 1 3 '16		

FOLLETT

First published in the United States, Great Britain, Canada,
Australia, and New Zealand in 1987 by North-South Books Inc.,
an imprint of NordSüd Verlag AG, Zürich, Switzerland.
First paperback edition published in 1994.

Distributed in the United States by North-South Books Inc., New York

Library of Congress Cataloging-in-Publication Data
Pfister, Marcus.
Penguin Pete
Translation of Penguin Pete.
Summary: Pete the Penguin has a good time playing on land with his
fellow birds and learning how to swim in the sea.
[1. Penguins–Fiction] 1. Title
PZ7.P448558Pe 1987
[E] 87-1627

A CIP catalogue record for this book is available from The British Library.

ISBN: 978-1-55858-018-3 (trade binding) 15 14 13
ISBN: 978-1-55858-356-6 (paperback) 10 9

Printed in Belgium

www.northsouth.com

Marcus Pfister

Penguin Pete

Translated by Anthea Bell

NORTHSOUTH
BOOKS

New York / London

Once upon a time there was a colony of penguins living happily together in the Antarctic. The youngest penguin was called Pete.

He was so small that the other penguins called him Pint-Sized Pete.

"Don't worry," said Pete's mother. "All penguins are pint-sized when they're young. One day you'll grow bigger, and then you'll be able to swim in the sea with the rest of us."

Pete thought the grown-up penguins looked beautiful swimming in the sea. He wanted to grow up fast so he could join them.

But when the penguins came back in the evening, and waddled clumsily to their nesting places, Pete couldn't help laughing. They looked so funny! Grown-up penguins couldn't move about on snow and ice any better than Pint-Sized Pete.

"I'll show them a penguin can move gracefully on land!" said Pete to himself. And he began practising flipper-skating every day. It was great fun! He slid about all over the ice, and usually ended up on the ground with a thump.

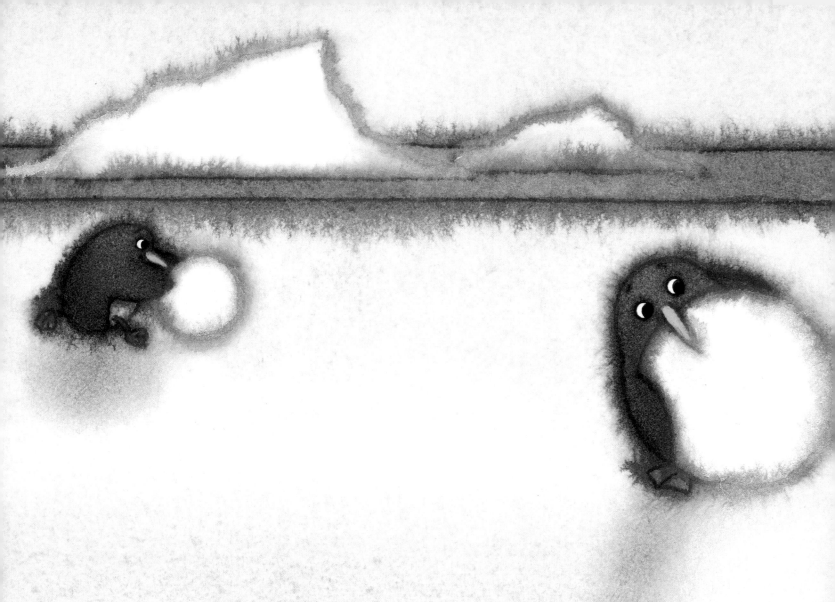

Now and then some of the other penguins who were
Pete's friends stayed home with him. Then they had a
wonderful time playing hide and seek, making snow penguins, and having snowball fights. The time flew by.

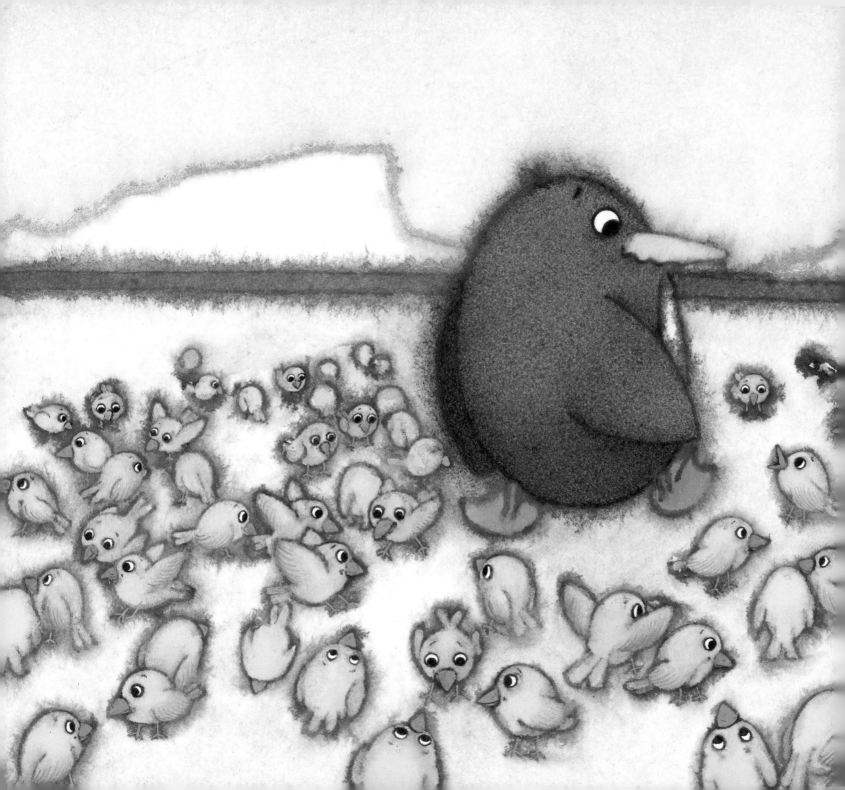

One day a flock of birds landed on the patch of ice where the penguins lived, calling and screeching and flapping their wings. Pete marched proudly through the rows of birds. How tiny they were! He felt very big and grown-up. "Hello!" said one of the little birds. "What kind of funny bird are you?"

"I'm a penguin," he said. "My name's Pete."

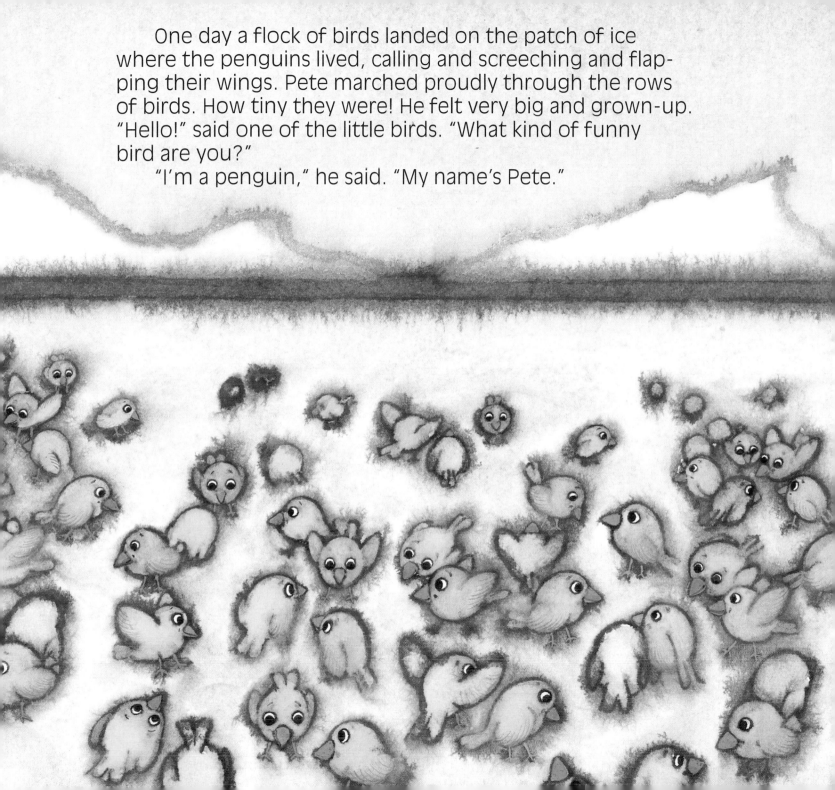

"Pleased to meet you, Pete!" said the little bird. "My name's Steve. Let's have a flying race!"

"Don't be silly," said Pete. "I can't fly."

"Then it's time you learned!" said Steve. "All you have to do is flap your wings hard. Just watch me! It's quite easy."

Pete tried and tried to fly, but he couldn't. He could only jump a little way into the air.

Pete and Steve were soon great friends, even if they couldn't go flying together.

But Pete wanted nothing better than to fly with his friend.

Although he tried to take off over and over again, his flights always ended in a crash landing.

The day came when the flock of birds had to move on. There was nothing Steve could do about it. As the two friends said goodbye, big penguin tears trickled down Pete's cheeks.

"Never mind, Pete," Steve called back as he flew away. "I'm sure we'll be landing on this patch of ice again next year."

Pete was very sad, but his mother knew how to cheer him up. The next morning he was allowed to go swimming in the sea for the first time.

He was very excited, though the thought of diving into the water head first was rather scary. But Pete found two ledges of ice at the water's edge. He climbed cautiously down the ledges and slid backwards into the sea.
"I'll do a proper dive tomorrow," thought Pete.

Pete's first few strokes were rather clumsy, but soon he was gliding through the cold water like an eel. He could even do a backstroke! He came in last in most of the swimming races, and he lost when the penguins played games, but Pete was a good loser.

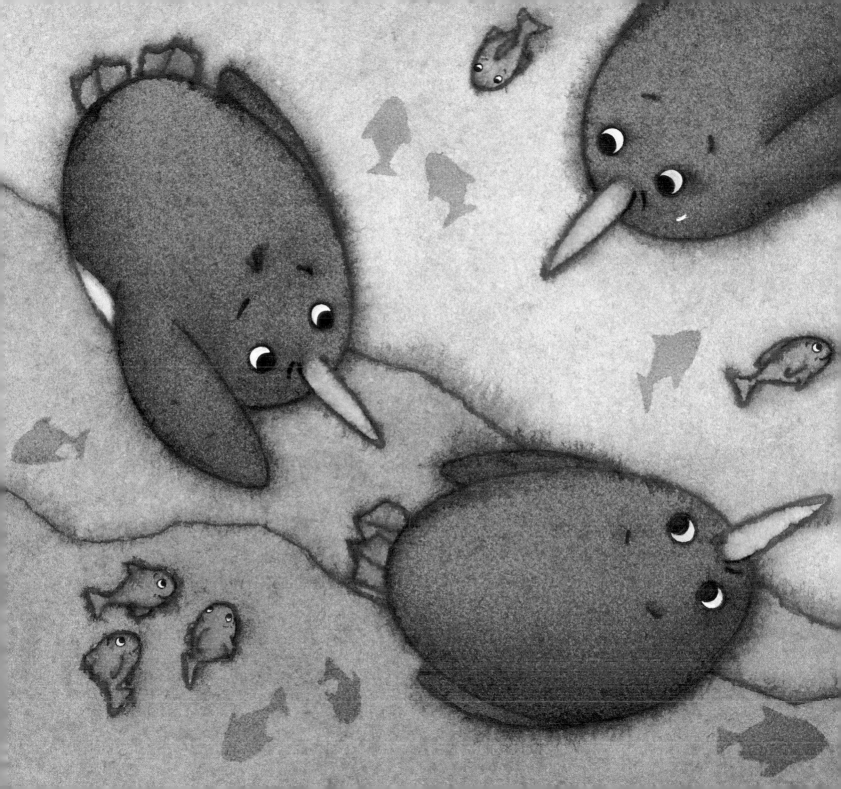

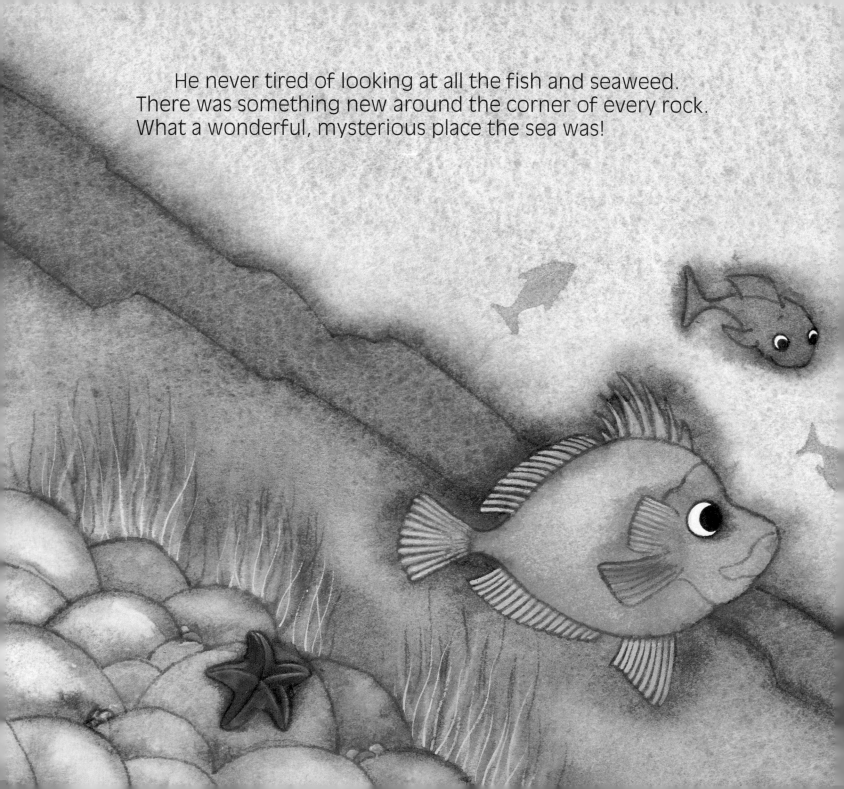

He never tired of looking at all the fish and seaweed.
There was something new around the corner of every rock.
What a wonderful, mysterious place the sea was!

The moon had risen by the time Pete waddled happily back to his mother. He felt far too tired to tell her about all his adventures, but that could wait until tomorrow.

He fell asleep at once, and dreamed of Steve, the sea, and the dive he was going to do next day.